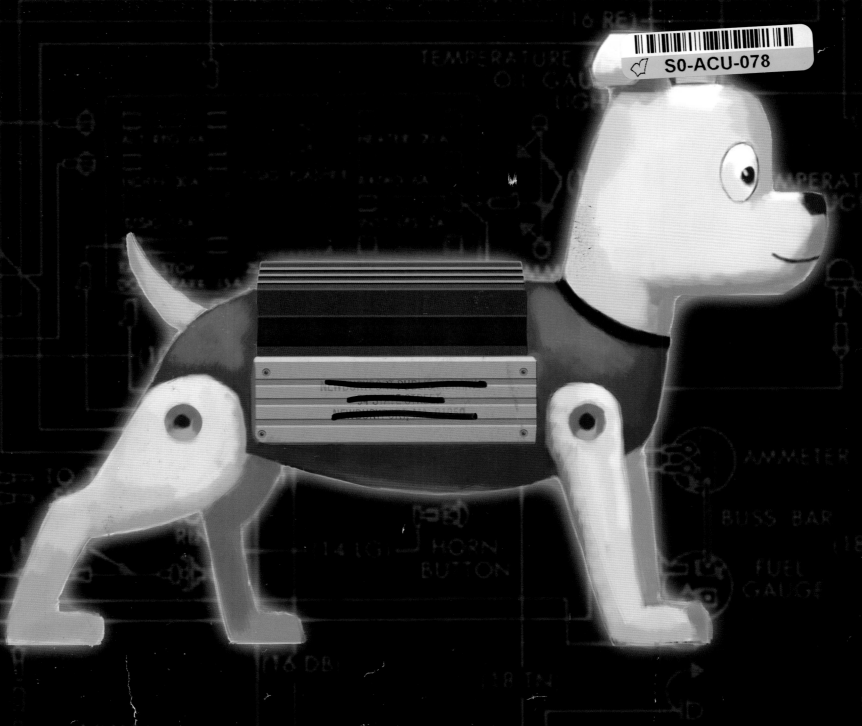

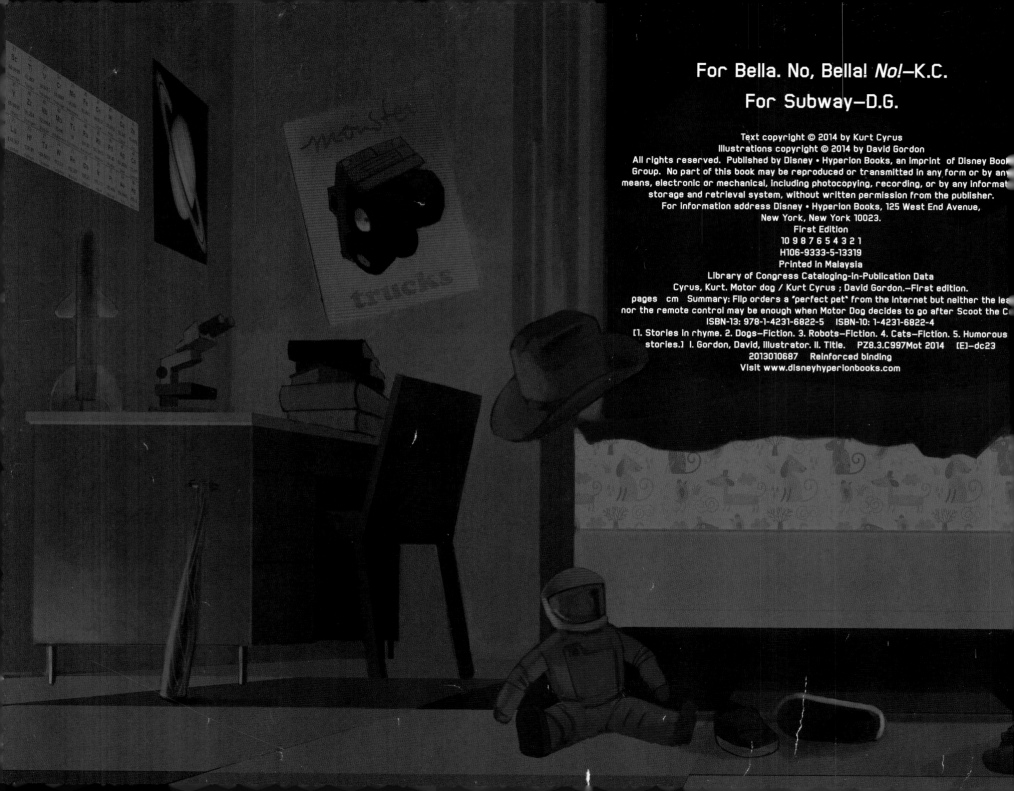

For Bella. No, Bella! *No!*—K.C.

For Subway—D.G.

Text copyright © 2014 by Kurt Cyrus
Illustrations copyright © 2014 by David Gordon
All rights reserved. Published by Disney • Hyperion Books, an imprint of Disney Book
Group. No part of this book may be reproduced or transmitted in any form or by any
means, electronic or mechanical, including photocopying, recording, or by any informat
storage and retrieval system, without written permission from the publisher.
For information address Disney • Hyperion Books, 125 West End Avenue,
New York, New York 10023.
First Edition
10 9 8 7 6 5 4 3 2 1
H106-9333-5-13319
Printed in Malaysia
Library of Congress Cataloging-in-Publication Data
Cyrus, Kurt. Motor dog / Kurt Cyrus ; David Gordon.—First edition.
pages   cm   Summary: Flip orders a "perfect pet" from the Internet but neither the lea
nor the remote control may be enough when Motor Dog decides to go after Scoot the C
ISBN-13: 978-1-4231-6822-5   ISBN-10: 1-4231-6822-4
[1. Stories in rhyme. 2. Dogs—Fiction. 3. Robots—Fiction. 4. Cats—Fiction. 5. Humorous
stories.] I. Gordon, David, illustrator. II. Title.   PZ8.3.C997Mot 2014   [E]—dc23
2013010687   Reinforced binding
Visit www.disneyhyperionbooks.com

Kurt Cyrus

David Gordon

MOTORDOG

Disney · HYPERION BOOKS
NEW YORK

Flip the Kid
found Motor Dog
by scrolling through
a catalog.

He clicked on *Buy* ...
then clicked on *Send* ...

...and just like that, he had a friend.

"Hey!" said Flip. "Remote control!"
He touched the pad and entered:

rocket
jet
walk
fetch
stroll

Ratchet-razzle-doink—PING!

Ratchet-razzle-doink—PING!

Across the lawn and down the street
went Motor Dog on bouncy feet.

Scoot the Cat.
Scoot the Cat.
On the curb he calmly sat.

Motor Dog went *bonkers* at
the sight of Scoot the Cat.

The robot pup
powered up.

Zip! Zing! Zing! Zip—

Motor Dog switched off his ears.
Then he lit his booster rocket.

Flip's right shoulder
left its socket.

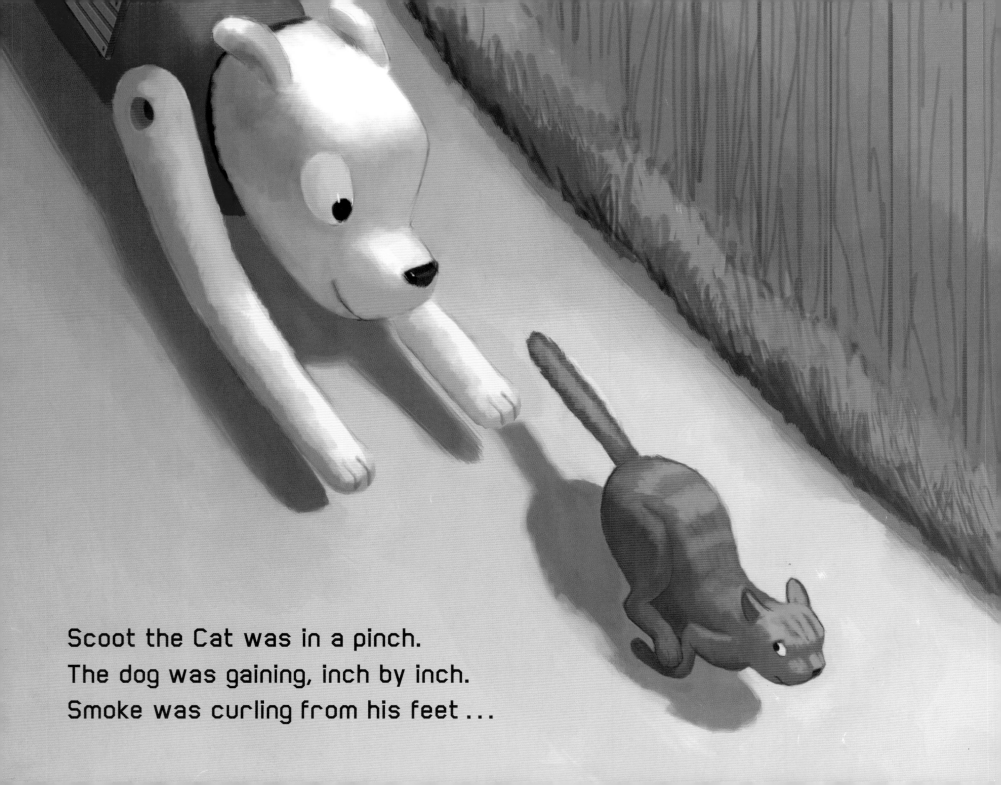

Scoot the Cat was in a pinch.
The dog was gaining, inch by inch.
Smoke was curling from his feet ...

"Quit!" said Flip. "Reboot! Delete!
Error! Error! Shutting down!"

Clocks blinked **twelve**
all over town.

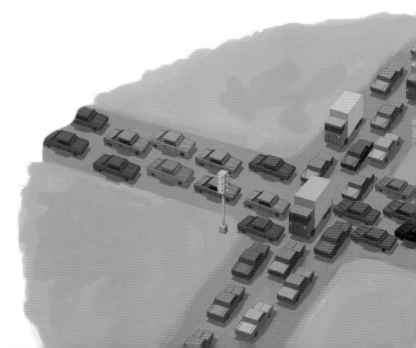

Motor Dog completely froze,
motionless from head to toes.

Then he started up again.

"On," said Flip. "All righty, then.

Enter password: one-two-three.

Motor Dog, you come with me."

Upward, upward
climbed the cat.

Scoot the Cat
just hissed and spat.

Motor Dog resumed attack.
"*Halt!*" said Flip. "You maniac!
Shift! Return! Undo! Unplug!"

Motor Dog went

Chug Chug Chug.

Scoot the Cat just scoffed at that.
Scoff! Scoff!
Hairball cough!
Springing like an acrobat,
up the branches leapt the cat.

Dog and boy went upward too.

Round and round the tree they flew,

zipping here
and zooming there,
signals flying everywhere.

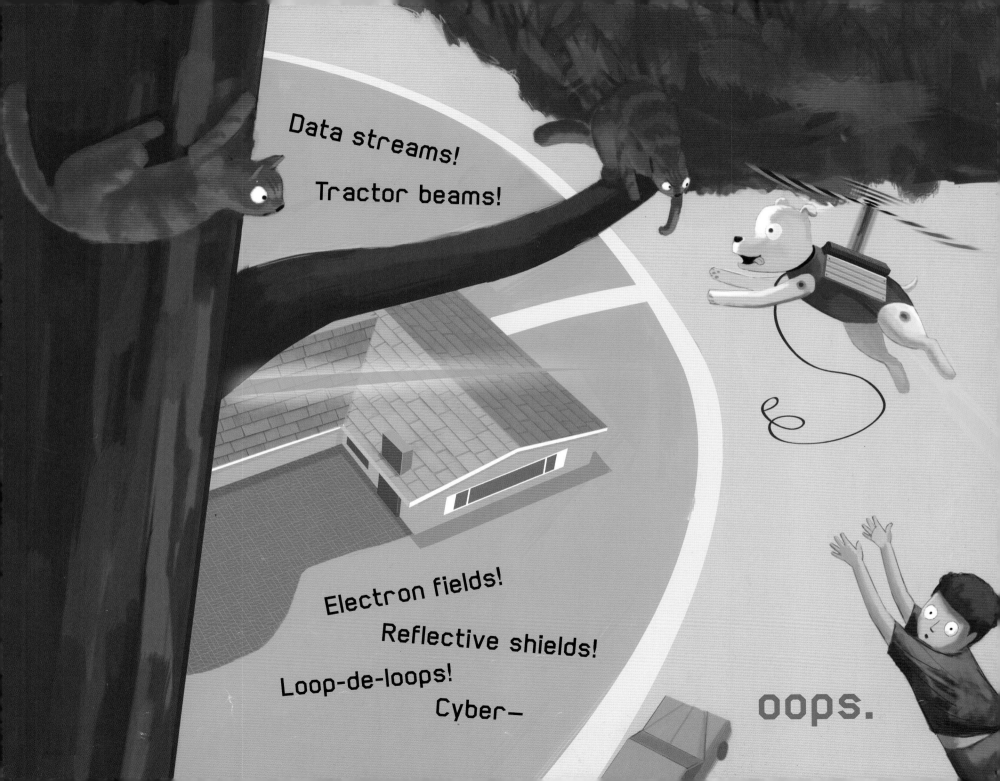

"On!" yelled Flip. "One-two-three!

Enter password!
Mercy me!

Slight malfunction! Minor glitch!
Upload? Download? Which is which?"

Flip the Kid was out of tricks.
Down he fell, toward the bricks.

The leash was loose. The dog was free,
and Scoot was cornered in the tree!
Through the limbs the puppy wove—

then like a rocket, **down** he dove!

He wasn't on a leash, it's true.
But still he stuck to Flip like glue,
their hearts connected with a string:
the bond of *love*—a wondrous thing!

(And some electrostatic cling.)

Chute deployed! Thrusters on! Easy landing on the lawn.

"This will never do," Flip stated. "Things are way too complicated. Bonus features? Extra stuff? Just a dog is good enough."

Flip shut off the high-tech gear,
scratched his dog behind the ear,
and gave his head a loving pat.
He called him "Buddy" after that....

WHOOSH! ZOOM! went Rocket Cat.

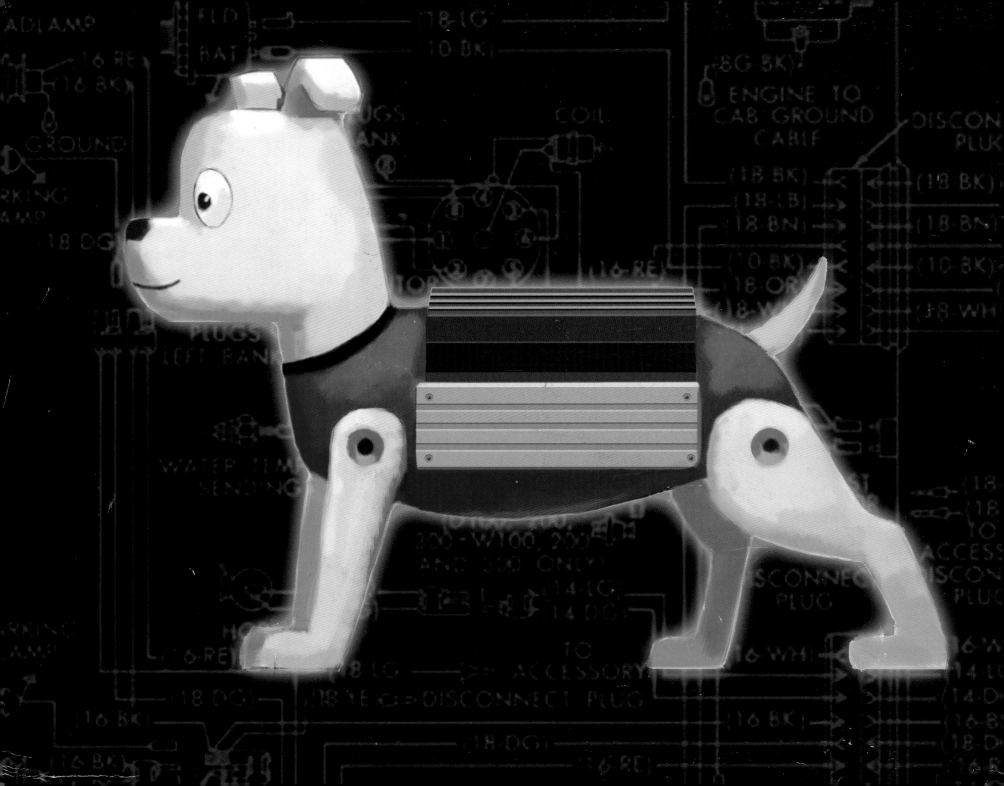